Written by Phil Vischer

Illustrated by Phil Dimitriadis and Chuck Vollmer

BIG IDEA
BOOKS

Zonderkidz

BIG IDEA
BOOKS®

www.bigidea.com

Zonder**kidz**®

The children's group of Zondervan
www.zonderkidz.com

A Snoodle's Tale
Copyright © 2004 by Big Idea Productions, Inc.
Illustrations copyright © 2004 by Big Idea Productions, Inc.

Requests for information should be addressed to:
Zonderkidz, Grand Rapids, Michigan 49530

ISBN: 0-310-70751-X

Written by: Phil Vischer
Editor: Cindy Kenney
Illustrated by: Big Idea Visual Development Artists

Printed in China
04 05 06 07/HK/4 3 2 1

"Hey kids! Have you ever had someone make you feel bad or say you're no good at anything?"

"We have a story that might help. It's called 'A Snoodle's Tale'."

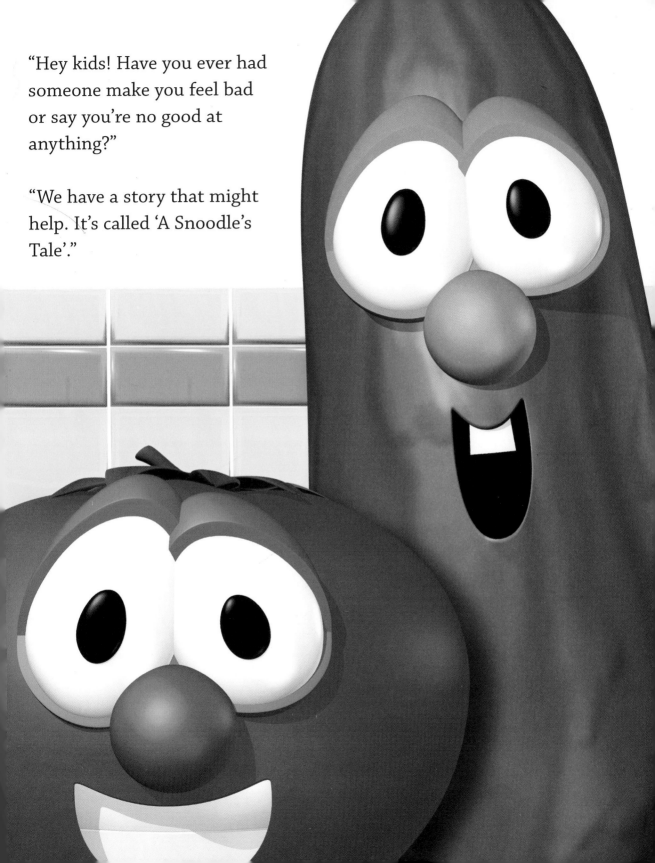

Far, far away in the land of Galoots,
Where the biggle-bag trees bear their biggle-bag fruits,
And far-lilly bushes all blossom in yellow,
And thimbuttle plants squirt snooberry Jell-O.

Here, where the mountains of Rocky-magoo,
Rise high over the meadows of Gilda-manjoo;
Where sunsets are painted with purple and blue,
You'll find a small town not much bigger than you.

Welcome to Snoodleburg! Home of the Snoodles!
A curious folk who eat pancakes with noodles.
And spend half their days making sketches and doodles,
And cutting their hair into shapes like French poodles.

Now, right in the heart of this curious town,
Is a curious building—the tallest around!
With a clock at its top and a chute at its bottom,
'Tis pink in the spring and turns red in the autumn.

But weirder by far than its color or height,
Is what happens there every fourth Tuesday night.
As strange as it seems, it has been demonstrated
That Snoodles aren't born, but rather, "created."

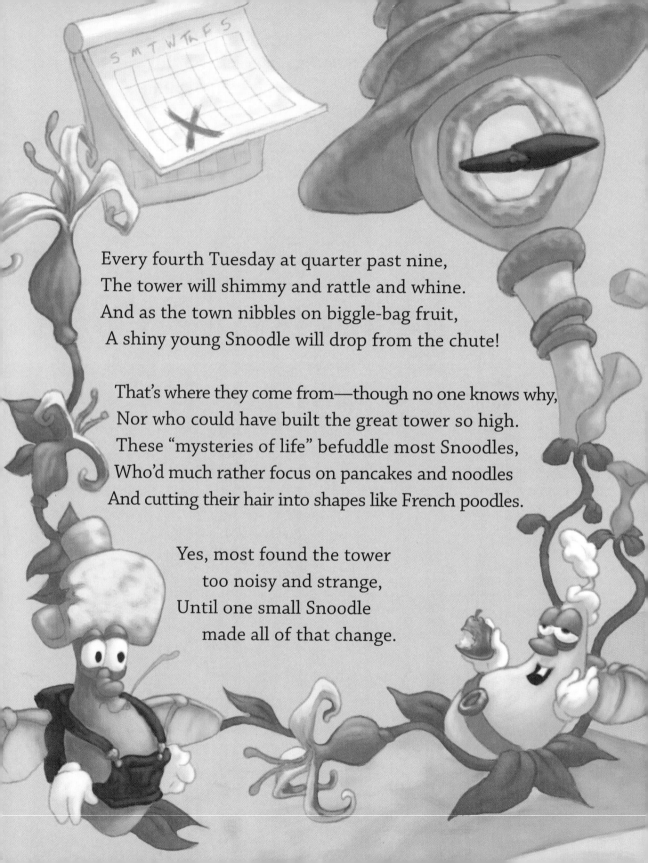

Every fourth Tuesday at quarter past nine,
The tower will shimmy and rattle and whine.
And as the town nibbles on biggle-bag fruit,
A shiny young Snoodle will drop from the chute!

That's where they come from—though no one knows why,
Nor who could have built the great tower so high.
These "mysteries of life" befuddle most Snoodles,
Who'd much rather focus on pancakes and noodles
And cutting their hair into shapes like French poodles.

Yes, most found the tower
too noisy and strange,
Until one small Snoodle
made all of that change.

This little Snoodle
was much like the others.
He came without siblings—
no sisters or brothers.
He came without money,
a mom or a dad.
The pack on his back
was all that he had.

"This is peculiar," the little guy said.
"I came from a chute, and I fell on my head.
What do I look like? What am I for?"
He pondered those questions—and then thought of more.

"Checking my bag is a good place to start."
He pulled out some paints. "Maybe I'm good at art!"
The next thing he found was a Snoodle-kazoo
"Hey, what do you know! I can make music too!"

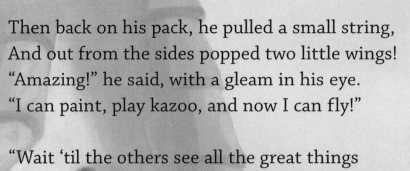

Then back on his pack, he pulled a small string,
And out from the sides popped two little wings!
"Amazing!" he said, with a gleam in his eye.
"I can paint, play kazoo, and now I can fly!"

"Wait 'til the others see all the great things
I can do with my paints, my kazoo, and my wings!"
So he packed up his paints, and his Snoodle-kazoo,
And hopped off to show them all what he could do.

There from the top of a short, stubby wall,
The big Snoodles heard the new small Snoodle call,
"Come watch me, you guys, as I head for the sky!"
He straightened his wings with a gleam in his eye.

Then he jumped and he flapped
like the Red-Snootered Finches
That fly from the plains to the peak of Mount Ginchez.
His flight—unlike theirs—covered only twelve inches.

"You call that flying? You think you're a bird?
We've never seen anything quite so absurd!"
The old Snoodle snorted—he sniggered, he shook.
"I'll paint you a picture to show how you looked!"

The brushstrokes were skillful; the colors were coolish.
The story they told made the young one feel foolish.
"Take it from us," said a Snoodle named Lou.
"Flying must not be what you're meant to do!"

The young Snoodle drooped. He felt his heart sag.
The painting, the old Snoodle placed in his bag.
"Carry this with you," the old Snoodle said,
"So visions of flying don't go to your head."
The weight on his back was as heavy as lead.

So under the weight of the picture he bore,
He hobbled along, feeling lonely and sore.
'Til up far ahead on a bench near the tower,
He spied a bright bundle of far-lilly flowers.

His heart started lifting. "What beautiful things!"
Then he remembered, "I've got more than wings!"
So quickly, he dug the paints out of his pack,
And hoped that with art—maybe he'd have a knack.

"I did it!" he yelled to the Snoodles in town,
Then held up his picture as they gathered round.
"You did it, all right," said the Snoodles replying.
"You showed you're no better at painting than flying!"

Then one of them laughed, and while eating a waffle,
Painted a picture that made him feel awful.
"You're puny. You're silly. You're not all that smart.
You can't use your wings, and you're no good at art."

That picture, too, was placed in his pack,
And made his heart slump just as low as his back.
"I'm ugly—I'm foolish—I'm so very small.
I don't think I should be with Snoodles at all."

And so he decided to get out of town.
His wings hung so low that they dragged on the ground.
He walked past the tower and out of the city.
He walked through the fields and thought: *My, this is pretty.*
The far-lilly bushes, all blooming in yellow,
And thimbuttle plants, squirting snooberry Jell-O.
"I might like it here," said the small Snoodle fellow.

Then feeling some warmth coming back in his chest,
He thought he would sit for a moment and rest.
But try as he might to sit down with grace,
The weight on his back knocked him flat on his face!

"Ha! That's a hoot!" said a voice from behind.
A farmer stood up with a thimbuttle vine.
"Why, you need a picture, my Snoodleburg bud,
Lest you forget how you look in the mud!"

And so in an instant, the picture was done,
And placed in his backpack, which now weighed a ton!
The poor Snoodle struggled, he wobbled, he groaned.
He stood to his feet and he said with a moan,
"Is there *anywhere* I can be truly alone?"

Just then overhead, flew two red-snootered finches
Winging their way toward the peak of Mount Ginchez.
"I see," said the Snoodle, "Then that's what I'll do.
The home for those finches will be my home too."

So painfully, struggling under his pack,
The small Snoodle inched up the big mountain's back.
He crawled over boulders in rain and in lightning.
He trudged on and on though the journey was frightening.

'Til finally Sunday at quarter past two,
He spied all the meadows of Gilda-manjoo
And realized he was on top of Mount Ginchez,
Alone with the wind, and his thoughts, and the finches.

He thought of the Snoodles. He thought of the tower.
He thought of the bell that would chime on the hour.
He thought of his pack and his very long walk.
He thought it so loudly, he heard his thoughts talk!

Hello, said his thoughts, *You've made quite a climb!*
"That voice," he remarked, "doesn't sound much like mine."
Then he turned, and he noticed he wasn't alone,
For a man stood behind near a cave in the stone.

He looked like a Snoodle, though quite a bit bigger.
Maybe a giant, the small Snoodle figured.
"I'm going!" the Snoodle boy said with a huff.
"And don't paint a picture—I've got quite enough!"

"But first come inside," the man said. "Have some tea!
I'm so very pleased that you're visiting me!"
The Snoodle boy stopped, though he'd only gone inches,
And stared at the stranger he'd found on Mount Ginchez.

He didn't seem angry, in fact, he looked kind.
The poor little boy was confused, "Are you *blind*?
I'm puny! I'm silly! I'm not all that smart!
I can't use my wings, and I'm no good at art!"
The stranger leaned down with a pain in his heart.

"Who told you these things?" he asked. "How do you know?"
"These pictures I have in my pack tell me so,"
The small Snoodle sniffled and started to go.

"First, if you please, let me look at this art
That makes your pack heavy and weighs down your heart."
Then picture by picture, he unpacked the bag
That bent the poor Snoodle and made his wings sag.

"Dear boy," said the man, "these look nothing like you!"
Then into the fire, the pictures he threw.
He rose from his chair, saying, "Wait there—you'll see
That what you need most is a picture from me!"

The Snoodle sat patiently, sipping his tea.

Then from a room in the back he returned,
Saying, "Dear little Snoodle, it's time that you learned
What you really look like!" And he threw off the sheet.
And what the boy saw warmed him right to his feet.

The boy in the portrait looked older and strong,
With wings on his back that were sturdy and long,
And a look in his eye, both courageous and free.
"Sir," asked the boy, "Are you saying that's—me?"

"I'd like to believe it, but, sir, I'm afraid to."
"I know who you are," the man said, "for I made you."

"I built the tower and set it in motion.
I planted the meadow—put fish in the ocean.
And I feed the finches, though most Snoodles doubt it,
Not one of them falls that I don't know about it."

"I've seen you fall down in the mud and the goo.
I've seen all you've done and all you will do.
I gave you your pack and your paints and your wings.
I chose them for you. They're your special things."

"The Snoodle-kazoo is so you can sing
About colors in autumn or flowers in spring.
I gave you your brushes in hopes that you'd see
How using them, you can make pictures for me."

"Most of the Snoodles," the old one said sadly,
"Just use their paints to make others feel badly."
The young Snoodle pondered the things he'd been told.
Then wondering something, grew suddenly bold.

"But sir, if you made this incredible land,
Can't you make Snoodles obey your command?"
The big one smiled warmly, then said to the small,
"A gift that's demanded is no gift at all."

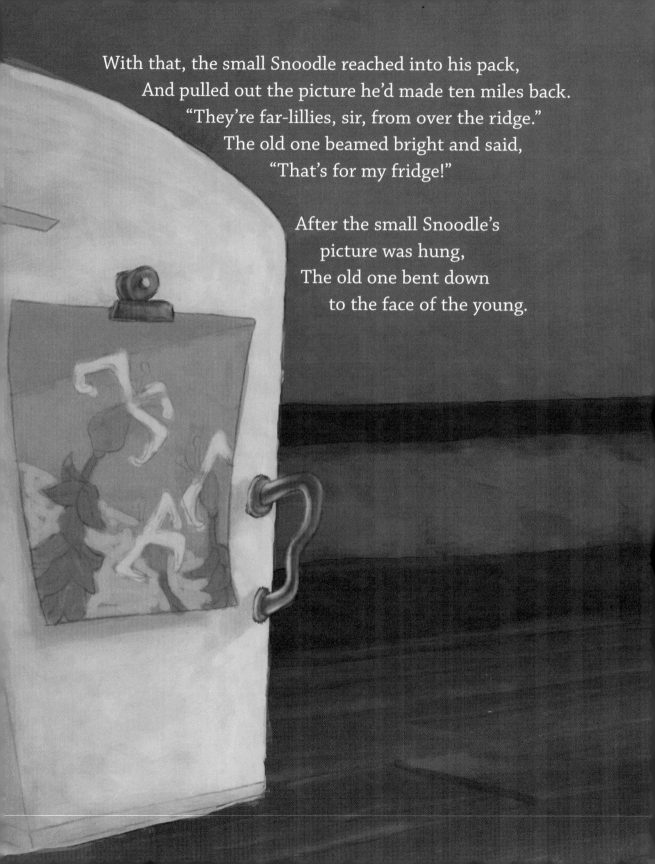

With that, the small Snoodle reached into his pack,
And pulled out the picture he'd made ten miles back.
"They're far-lillies, sir, from over the ridge."
The old one beamed bright and said,
"That's for my fridge!"

After the small Snoodle's
picture was hung,
The old one bent down
to the face of the young.

He said, "Here's what you look like; Here's how I see you.
Keep this in your pack, and you'll find it will free you
From all of the pictures and all of the lies
That others make up just to cut down your size."

"And lastly, your wings. You know what they're for!
But not just to fly, son, I want you to soar!"

"But sir," said the Snoodle, "how can I fly?
This picture's so big, I won't get very high!"

"But this picture's special—it's bigger, it's brighter.
Carry it close, and I think you'll feel lighter."

As soon as he heard it, the Snoodle looked down,
And noticed his feet were an inch off the ground!
He laughed and he leaped and he ran from the cave,
Feeling now older and stronger and brave.

He flew through the clouds,
and he flew with the finches.
He soared up and down
'round the peak of Mount Ginchez.
He flew over far-lilly bushes in yellow,
And thimbuttle plants squirting snooberry Jell-O.

He flew over biggle-bag trees and their fruits,
In big, lazy loops o'er the land of Galoots.
Then hurried back home to the center of town,
Where the Snoodles all stood with their wings on the ground.

And starting precisely at quarter past two,
He told them the story that I just told you.

"So you see? Once we know how God sees us, it doesn't matter what anyone else says.

Until next time, remember— God made you special, and he loves you very much!"